This book belongs to ...

....

Tips for Talking and Reading Together

Stories are an enjoyable and reassuring way of introducing children to new experiences.

Before you read the story:

- Talk about the title and the picture on the cover. Ask your child what they think the story might be about.
- Talk about what it's like to keep a pet. Has your child ever kept a pet?

Read the story with your child. After you have read the story:

- Discuss the Talk About ideas on page 27.
- Go through the instructions for looking after a pet rabbit on pages 28 – 29.
- Do the fun activity on page 30.

Have fun!

Find the carrots hidden in every picture.

For more hints and tips on helping your child become a successful and enthusiastic reader look at our website www.oxfordowl.co.uk.

Kipper's First Pet

Written by Roderick Hunt
and Annemarie Young
Illustrated by Alex Brychta

OXFORD

UNIVERSITY PRESS

Kipper went to play with Anna. Anna's brother was called Al. He had two rabbits called Tina and Tess.

"Tess is rather fat," said Kipper.

Al let Kipper stroke Tess. The rabbit felt soft and warm.
Its nose went up and down.

"She likes you," said Anna.

"The rabbits are fun," said Al, "but we can't go on holiday. There's nobody to look after them."

"We can do that," said Kipper.

Mum came to take Kipper home.

"I told Anna and Al that we can look after the rabbits," said Kipper. "So now they can go on holiday."

"Well," said Mum. "You should have asked me first. And you will have to look after them."

"I will," said Kipper.

A week later, Anna and Al came with Tina and Tess.
Anna's dad had the hutch and all the things the rabbits
would need.

Kipper felt nervous. He didn't know how to look after rabbits. He looked at Biff and Chip.

"Will you help me?" he asked.

Anna's dad set up the hutch by the shed.

"This is a cool place," he said. "It's out of the sun."

"This tray goes in their hutch," said Al. "Put newspaper
in it, with hay on top. This is what the rabbits sleep on."

"The paper gets really wet, so change it every day," said Anna.

"Ugh!" said Biff. "What a job! Kipper can do that."

"Rabbits like hay most of all," said Anna, "but they also like a few carrots or cabbage leaves. And give them lots of water to drink."

Floppy was shut inside, but Dad opened the door.

Floppy ran out and barked at the rabbits.

"Sorry!" said Dad. "I forgot."

The next day, Kipper went to see the rabbits, but Tina wasn't there! She had dug a hole under the wire.

Kipper saw Tina by the tree.

"Don't run away," said Kipper.

He went up to Tina very slowly and held her gently.

Suddenly, Floppy ran out again.

Biff and Chip grabbed Floppy. They called Dad, and he ran to help Kipper.

"Well done!" said Dad.

"Well!" said Dad. "That mustn't happen again."

"It's hard work looking after rabbits," said Kipper.

The rabbits needed more hay, so Dad took Biff, Chip and Kipper to the pet shop.

"Look at this parrot," said Chip.

"Do you keep the rabbits outside?" asked the man.
"There are going to be fireworks tonight. The rabbits will
be scared."

Kipper was worried about the fireworks, so Dad put the rabbits inside. Kipper gave the rabbits extra bedding to snuggle down in.

BOOM! BANG! went the fireworks.

"Poor rabbits!" said Kipper.

After their long holiday, Anna and Al came to take the rabbits home.

"Thank you," said Anna's dad, "but why is the hutch inside?"

"We have a surprise," said Kipper.

"Tess wasn't just fat. She's had six baby rabbits!"

"I don't believe it!" said Al.

"Would you like one of the babies when they get bigger?" asked Anna.

"No thank you," said Kipper. "It's hard work looking after rabbits!"

Talk about the story

Why did Kipper say he'd look after the rabbits?

What do rabbits like to eat most of all?

How did Kipper feel when he was looking after the rabbits?

Talk about a pet you'd like to look after.

27

How to look after pet rabbits

Rabbits like company. It's best to have more than one.

Hutches need two compartments – one for the rabbits during the day and one for nesting at night.

Put the hutch where it's sheltered in winter and shady in summer.

The rabbits sleep in their nest box, with newspaper and hay on top. Change the straw and paper every day.

Give the rabbits clean, fresh water to drink every day.

Rabbits eat mainly hay, but they also like a few carrots, and cabbage or lettuce leaves to nibble.

Rabbits need plenty of exercise. Give them somewhere safe to run about.

Rabbits don't like to be picked up too often. They like to be stroked.

Spot the pair

Find the two baby rabbits that are exactly the same.

FIRST EXPERIENCES WITH Biff, Chip & Kipper

Have you read them all yet?

Kipper's First Pet

Learning to Swim

Going to the Dentist

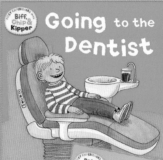

Fun at the Farm

Going to the Doctor

Going to the Hairdresser

Going on a Plane

series created by Roderick Hunt and Alex Brychta

Starting School

FIRST EXPERIENCES Flashcards
55 cards

Also available:
- **Kipper Gets Nits!**
- **At the Hospital**
- **At the Optician**
- **Bottles, Cans, Plastic Bags**
- **On a Train**
- **At the Vet**
- **At the Match**
- **At the Dance Class**

Read with Biff, Chip and Kipper
The UK's best-selling home reading series

Phonics

First Stories

	Phonics	First Stories
Level 1 Getting ready to read		
Level 2 Starting to read		
Level 3 Becoming a reader		
Level 4 Developing as a reader		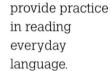
Level 5 Building confidence in reading		
Level 6 Reading with confidence		

Phonics stories help children practise their sounds and letters, as they learn to do in school.

First stories have been specially written to provide practice in reading everyday language.

READ WITH Biff, Chip & Kipper

OXFORD
UNIVERSITY PRESS

Great Clarendon Street, Oxford OX2 6DP
Text © Roderick Hunt and Annemarie
Young 2007
Illustrations © Alex Brychta 2007
First published 2007
This edition published 2012

10 9 8 7 6 5 4 3 2 1
Series Editors: Kate Ruttle, Annemarie Young
British Library Cataloguing in Publication Data available
ISBN: 978-0-19-848792-0
Printed in China by Imago